Romeo and Me

PRAISE FOR *STORYSHARES*

"One of the brightest innovators and game-changers in the education industry."
– Forbes

"Your success in applying research-validated practices to promote literacy serves as a valuable model for other organizations seeking to create evidence-based literacy programs."

- Library of Congress

"We need powerful social and educational innovation, and Storyshares is breaking new ground. The organization addresses critical problems facing our students and teachers. I am excited about the strategies it brings to the collective work of making sure every student has an equal chance in life."
– Teach For America

"Around the world, this is one of the up-and-coming trailblazers changing the landscape of literacy and education."
- International Literacy Association

"It's the perfect idea. There's really nothing like this. I mean wow, this will be a wonderful experience for young people."   - Andrea Davis Pinkney, Executive Director, Scholastic

"Reading for meaning opens opportunities for a lifetime of learning. Providing emerging readers with engaging texts that are designed to offer both challenges and support for each individual will improve their lives for years to come. Storyshares is a wonderful start."
- David Rose, Co-founder of CAST & UDL

Romeo and Me

Jennie Ford

STORYSHARES

Story Share, Inc.
New York. Boston. Philadelphia

Published in the United States by Story Share, Inc.

The characters and events in this book are fictitious. Any similarity to real persons, living or dead, is entirely coincidental.

Storyshares
Story Share, Inc.
24 N. Bryn Mawr Avenue #340
Bryn Mawr, PA 19010-3304
www.storyshares.org

Inspiring reading with a new kind of book.

Interest Level: Middle School
Grade Level Equivalent: 4.8

9781642611779

Book design by Storyshares

Printed in the United States of America

Storyshares Presents

1

"Until lions tell their tale, the story of the hunt will always glorify the hunter." ~ African Proverb

Romeo and I were best, best friends. We grew up together as far back as I can remember. We were barn babies, wrapped in quilts and laid in an empty, wooden trailer at sunrise, where we would sleep until the sun warmed our faces, and the dew began to dry. We rose to the sounds of tractors rolling in from the fields, and the barn ladies talking and laughing. We woke to the smell of dust and the cigarettes the barn men smoked. We opened our eyes to old pine limbs above us, blowing slowly on a lazy breeze.

I went to the barn every morning with Papa, my grandfather, and Romeo, along with his mama, Rowena. It was my Papa's tobacco farm, and he was stuck with me. My Granny worked at the sewing factory in town, and my sister, Suzanne, went to Great-grannys house. There she sat in front of a big fan and watched television with Great-granny and ate egg salad sandwiches. I didn't like staying with her, and I am pretty sure Great-granny didn't like me staying there, either, so Papa was stuck with me.

Romeo's mama worked at the tobacco barns every summer, and he didn't have anywhere to go either, so here we stayed. We liked it. We had very few rules. We knew not to climb on the big piles of the long, wooden sticks that the ladies tied the tobacco leaves to, for fear of black widow spiders, or copperhead snakes hiding in them. We knew to stay out of the way of the workers, or we'd get a scolding,or worse. Our biggest rule was not to get run over by a tractor or backed over by the trailers that hauled the big, green, sticky leaves from the field to the barns.

Upon waking, we would find our wrinkled brown bags that held our breakfast (usually an apple, a jar of milk, a boiled egg and biscuit). We would eat and plan our day. Our summers were long and hot. Many days we found ourselves under a shady tree finding shapes in the clouds, or telling stories. Romeo was the best at telling tales. He recalled the stories his mother told him of Jonah and the whale, of David and Goliath. Stories of the Bible that I knew nothing of. My favorite stories were the ones told to him by his Grandmother Von, stories of kings and queens. Of African kings and queens.

On one particular day, we laid on our backs in the shade. We felt cool and sleepy in the late afternoon.

"Tell me the stories Granny Von tells you, Romeo," I said.

With a big grin and sleepy eyes, he started, "There was once a strong and powerful young boy who went to battle with his father. His name was Hannibal. He was only 8 years old but fought for his people. He was made king when he was young and had a great army to defend his land. He used elephants to trample his enemies. He was a brave and strong and a smart warrior."

"How big are elephants?" I asked.

"Much bigger than the tractor," he said.

I thought about this and later we woke to the sounds of the workers coming in from the fields, their long days over.

"Okay, we will start again early in the morning before the heat sets in. It's been a good day," Papa said.

The workers, covered in the black tar of the green leaves, sat and fanned themselves with their hands, sweat pouring. They bade each other well until morning. Then Papa helped me gather my things and put me in his truck.

"Bye, Romeo," I waved.

"Bye, Caroline," he said.

Papa and I went home to where my Granny would immediately place me in the bath tub. The days dust and dirt was scrubbed off me, and my hair washed.

2

It took us no time at all to color every single picture in Romeo's new coloring book. We had given all the workers many pictures as gifts. They promised to take them home and hang them up, and told us they would think of us every time they looked at our lovely art work. That made us both grin with pride.

"Tomorrow, don't forget to bring something we can dig with," Romeo told me.

"I won't forget," I said.

Our plans were made. The best castle ever would be built. We were inspired by Granny Von's stories of a great king. A king who was the richest man in all the world. He built great castles decorated with silver and gold. His name was Mansa Musa.

* * *

The next morning Romeo ran to me. "Did you bring it?"

"Yes!" I reached into my bag and brought out Granny's garden spade and my sand bucket. "What did you bring?" I asked.

Romeo smiled and reached into his bag. He brought out shiny gold and silver tinsel meant for a Christmas tree.

"Beautiful," I said.

We had already staked out the site for our palace. It was a sandy area behind a pine thicket, still within view of his mama. We dug and dug.

We made tall towers with long sticks stuck in the top. I imagined ribboned flags atop, fluttering in the wind.

We made small, mounded houses around the castle which housed the people of the great kingdom.

Romeo took the tinsel from his bag and draped it all around the great palace. The tinsel sparkled in the sun. It was magical. Miss Rowena stopped her work to come look upon our creation.

"What have you kids done?" she asked, smiling.

"It is the palace of King Mansa Musa!" Romeo beamed. Rowena looked on our creation. Her hands went to her mouth. She smiled to her son.

"It is a fine palace," she said.

3

The hot summer wore on. We never failed to come up with a game or project to keep us busy. Some days it was enough just to sit under a shady tree and play *I spy*, or draw grand murals in the sand with sticks. Other times we sat and pondered about other places, what they must be like, such as the cold Alaska, or the jungles of Africa. We wondered about living with tigers and lions and elephants. We mused about the stars and the moon, and thunder and lightning and clouds.

Our young minds stayed busy, but we rarely thought about our here and now. We rarely thought about what would become of us and our futures. Those thoughts never crossed our minds; we were happy. We were innocent.

"I brought us a surprise today!" I said, running with my bag to Romeo.

"Let's see!" he said. I pulled out a large pad of paper, crayons and pencils.

"We can draw whatever we want," I told him.

"I already know what I'm going to draw," he said.

We found our spot under the shady tree and set out the supplies. Romeo began drawing. When he was done, he showed me. It was a lady with long red robes and a yellow crown. Her hair was black and her skin was brown.

"She's beautiful, Romeo," I told him.

"This is Queen Amina. She was called Amina, meaning woman as capable as man. She was a great leader of her country... she led an army of twenty thousand soldiers. She built giant walled cities and ruled for many, many years."

"She was brave," I say. "I love your stories."

Romeo and Me

4

Summer was coming quickly to an end. On the last day of work, Papa would cook chickens on the grill, and all the workers brought food. It was a day of celebration for all - all but me and Romeo.

When summer ended, we knew we would see very little of each other before the next season. Occasionally, we met in the general store, or waved out the windows when we passed on the road. But it wasn't the same. The magic we had at the barns wasn't there. It left an empty spot in the very pit of my stomach. I guess that's what missing someone feels like.

We heard the hoots and hollers of the people playing a game of horseshoes, and the ladies swapping recipes and bragging about the food. Romeo and I sat in the swing on my front porch with our heads down.

The cars and pickup trucks were loaded and everyone hugged and said their goodbyes.

"Romeo, it's time to go," his father, Marcus said. "Why such sad faces, you two?" he asked.

"I'm going to miss Caroline," Romeo answered slowly.

His father looked at the both of us and he seemed kind of bothered, too.

"You'll be seeing Miss Caroline, it'll be okay," he smiled.

It was a sad smile, I thought, if there is such a thing.

5

"It takes a village to raise a child."

- African Proverb

"Why, you two have done went and grown a foot a piece!" Miss Sarah exclaimed. She worked with Papa every summer. She looked the same year after year; always wearing a red kerchief to tie her hair back and a long-sleeved denim shirt, worn soft and faded.

Romeo and I stared at each other, shy at first. He had already turned six in the spring, and with my birthday coming, I was almost six as well. We had changed. We had lost the pudginess in our cheeks, his a soft brown and mine a pale pink. We were taller and lankier, but he was taller by far. We sat in an empty trailer, dangling our legs over the side.

"I heard your daddy moved up north for work," I said.

"He moved up there last month with Uncle Ronald. Hes working in a factory, and I sure miss him," Romeo replied. "But, he's coming home this weekend to see us. I can't wait." He smiled.

After a time, Romeo turned and asked me, "Where's your Mama and Daddy, Caroline?"

"I don't know where my daddy is. Mama, last I heard, she was living at the beach... she don't visit much." I thought about the last thing I just said. "Romeo, she don't visit none." That made me feel sad and guilty all at the same time, like I wasn't good enough for her to love.

"Well, you have a bad mama and daddy, that's what I say," Romeo said seriously. "Mamas and daddies are supposed to love their children...yes they are," he added.

I felt my eyes burn and lowered my head.

"Caroline, I'm sorry, I didn't mean to make you cry."

"You didn't, Romeo, and you're right. Mamas are supposed to love their children. I don't know why mine don't."

"I don't know either...I surely don't." Romeo shook his head side to side.

I put my face in my hands and Romeo put his thin little arm around my shoulders. Miss Rowena noticed us from the barn and walked to us. She knelt in front of me.

"What's wrong, baby?" she asked softly.

"I wish I had a mama like you," I sobbed. She hugged my neck and patted my head. She smelled of a soft soap.

"Why, Caroline, your mama ain't here, but you have so many people that love you. We love you, and your sweet Granny loves you, and I know your Papa would fight a bear for you! She held my face in her hands and smiled.

"Don't ever think that you ain't loved, never. Okay?" she smiled.

"Okay."

"Now you two get out here and play. You don't need to spend not one minute being sad over anything," Rowena told us.

"Yes, ma'am," I said. I felt better.

Rowena stood to leave and turned back to me. "My Mama used to tell me that it takes a village to raise a child. We are your village, Caroline," Rowena said.

It took me many years to understand what she told me, but slowly it made sense. I loved the people of my village. I still do.

6

It was Friday and Romeo was so excited. His daddy was on his way home for a long weekend. His family was planning a big celebration for him and his Uncle Ronald's return.

"Mama is going to ask your Papa if you can come to our celebration," Romeo told me as soon as we got to the barn.

"She is? I would love to!"

We were extra quiet and good that day. I watched as Miss Rowena talked to Papa. She promised to pick me up and bring me home and watch over me. Papa didn't hesitate when he told her I could attend.

Granny scrubbed me and dressed me in my best sundress. She pulled my hair into a ponytail and washed my shoes. She reminded me of my manners (yes sir, yes ma'am), and told me not to be a glutton. She told me to act like a young lady.

Miss Rowena and Romeo picked me up. Their house was set back off the road in a thicket of tall magnolia trees. The sweet smell of the magnolia blooms made me feel welcome. There were cars and trucks lined up their drive, and the sounds of laughter made me smile. In the backyard, several tables were set up full of covered dishes of food. Three grills were smoking, with men tending to the chickens and ribs. The smell was enough to make my mouth water and mystomach growl.

The older men and ladies sat in lawn chairs under the abundant shade trees in his yard. The younger people spread bright quilts on the lawn, spotting the yard with much color.

Romeo and I went straight to his tire swing, where we took turns seeing how high we could go.

"Romeo, aren't you going to introduce me to your guest?"

I looked and saw a tall, regal lady. She wore a dark, orange tunic and a yellow skirt. She had a beautiful, brightly colored scarf wrapped and knotted on her head. Her face was kind and her features looked as though they were sculpted from a soft brown stone. Romeo jumped off the swing and went over and wrapped both his arms around her waist.

"Grandmother!" he yelled in excitement. She hugged him back and kissed the top of his head.

"Grandmother, this is my best friend, Caroline," he said.

"Caroline, it is so great to meet you," she said, and took my hand. "I have heard so much about you."

"I have heard much about you, too. I love your stories."

"Oh, my stories... those stories are a part of the history of his people," she said, looking at Romeo. "It makes me happy that he shares them. Now, come on with me, the Reverend James is about to speak. Let's find a place to sit. Grandmother Von found a lawn chair, and Romeo and I sat on the ground at her feet.

The Reverend James was dressed in black pants, black shoes, and a white, long sleeved dress shirt. He wore black framed glasses and was big and tall. When he spoke, his voice was low and strong. He had a friendly face that smiled often. He stood and everyone quieted to listen.

"I want to thank you, Rowena, for asking me here today for this homecoming. Welcome home Marcus and Ronald, even if it is for a short time. As you can see by this beautiful celebration, you have been missed. Rowena asked me to say a prayer before we partake in this grand feast. I don't take this request lightly, no sir. I have reached into my soul to try to understand the love these family and friends have for you men; you men that have left your loving homes to better provide for your loved ones. That's a sacrifice, it is. I respect you and God blesses you. Let us pray."

The good Reverend prayed for the strength and safety of Mr. Marcus and Ronald. He prayed for them and all in attendance and asked God to keep us safe in His arms. His words made me feel special. He was praying for me. That felt good.

"Romeo, take Caroline in the house so she can wash her hands, and you wash yours, too. It's time to eat," Miss Rowena yelled over to us, while carrying out more food.

Romeo's house was much like my own, just another farm house. Something was different-feeling, though...it seemed warmer. I walked into his living room and one whole wall was hung with family pictures. Most were of Romeo - as a baby, a toddler, with his grandmother, his parents. A larger one stood out, one that wasn't Romeo. I peered at the man inside. He looked kind. He looked smart.

"Is this your Grandfather?" I asked.

"Which one?" he asked. I pointed. "No,that's Dr. King."

"Who is he?" I asked. Romeo smiled and said, "He is another African leader, but he don't lead with armies, he leads with peace."

"Kids?" Rowena yelled from the back door, "Let's eat!"

Romeo and Me

7

The celebration was ending. The ladies had worked themselves hard serving and cleaning and putting up food. Miss Rowena looked tired. She gave me a chocolate pie to take home to my family and said we would be leaving soon. Romeo and I waited for her at the car. We held hands and swung them while we sang a song.

"Hey, Ro," Marcus yelled to his son. He had been watching us.

"Hey, Daddy!"

"Why don't you stay here with me while your mama runs Miss Caroline home."

"Oh, okay, daddy. Is that okay with you?" he asked me.

"That's fine," I say.

It was almost dark when I got home. Papa and Granny were sitting on the porch, searching for a coolbreeze. They waved to Rowena as she pulled out of our long, sandy drive.

"Miss Rowena sent a chocolate pie," I said. "It was a fine day. Reverend James blessed me and I met Grandmother Von." I noticed my sister, Suzanne, at the screen door.

"Well, I'm not eating that pie," she said.

"It's good, I had some," I tell her.

"It was made by colored people. It's dirty," she said.

I looked to Papa, confused.

"Well, I'm gonna have me a piece," he said.

"Me, too," Granny added.

* * *

Miss Rowena and Romeo didn't come to work that Monday. They were spending one last day with Mr. Marcus before he had to leave. When they returned on Tuesday, I was so excited to see them.

"Romeo, you're back!" I ran to him before he could get out of the car. He smiled, but it wasn't the same.

"Are you okay?" I asked. "Are you missing your daddy?"

"Yes, I'm missing him awful. I wish he didn't have to leave. But that's not all," he said.

"What is it?" I ask.

"Daddy told me I can't be so close to you... he told me we can't be holding hands and hugging. He says I could get in trouble, that people might talk. That people might not understand."

"What? What people?" I ask.

"White people," he said. "Your people."

Romeo and Me

8

After that sad week, Romeo was sent to stay with his Grandmother Von in Raleigh for the remainder of the summer. I didn't know what to do with myself anymore. Me and Romeo had been together for as long back as I could remember. I sat under a shady tree and held my head low.

Some days, Papa would let me ride with him on the tractor to the fields where the workers plucked the tobacco leaves from their stalks and loaded them in the trailer.

"I don't like coming here no more, Papa," I told him.

"I know it's not the same without your friend," he said.

Some days Rowena would bring me to the barn and try to teach me how to tie the tobacco onto the wooden sticks. She let me stay with her and the barn ladies, shushing anyone that said something a young girl shouldn't hear.

"When will Romeo come back?" I asked her. She looked at me long and hard.

"His daddy thinks it would be good for him to stay in Raleigh this summer. He loves his Grandmother Von, you know. Before you know it, first grade will be starting! Are you excited, Caroline?"

"Is it because I'm white, Miss Rowena? Is that why he can't see me?"

"You don't... he don't..." she stumbled for words. "Caroline, you have wonderful grandparents, and they have raised you with no hate in your heart. The world out there... it isn't like it is on this farm. One day you will understand, and I hope you still feel the way you do now," she told me.

"Are you still my village, Miss Rowena?"

"Yes, I am," she said.

9

"In the end, we will remember not the words of our enemies, but the silence of our friends."

~ Martin Luther King, Jr.

Granny had worked until late every night, sewing school dresses for me. I got used to the sound of the sewing machine and it seemed to soothe me to sleep. I hadn't seen Romeo all summer and I wondered how he was.

Now, school started in two days, I was hoping to see him then. I wanted to ask him how Grandmother Von was doing. I wanted to ask him if she told him new stories. If it weren't for seeing him, I wouldn't want to go to school. In my heart I'd rather run the sandy fields and draw pictures in the sand. I'd rather watch the clouds take shape and dream and sleep and hear Grandmother Von's stories. But that wasn't to be anymore.

Bus number 73 would take me off this sandy land to a place called Lee County Elementary School. It was time to just accept it.

The first day of school, I looked and looked for Romeo. He wasn't in my class but I saw him in the lunch room. I waved a silly hello and saw a smile in his eyes, but he turned his head. Patsy Parker sat beside me.

"You waving to that colored boy?" She asked.

"That's my friend, Romeo," I told her. She whispered to Tammy Cameron next to her, and they got their trays and moved away.

The days went on and I quit waving to Romeo. I quit looking for Romeo. I settled into the normal. I settled into the girls who made fun of the people that had dirty clothes, the people who smelled of an old wood stove, the people who weren't just like us. I had many friends. I fit in to the people that judged and made fun of others. Others like Cheryl Bass who wore hand-me-downs that were much too big, like the colored kids, like Phillip Thomas who limped with cerebral palsy. I had many friends.

School taught me my abcs. School taught me intolerance.

Miss Rowena was right, the world was different off the farm. The world was bad.

I rode bus 73 and Romeo rode bus 7. We had to stand out and wait at the same place every day. I heard a ruckus and turned to look. One of the Kelly boys was picking on Romeo.

"Where did you get them fancy pants, black boy?" David Kelly yelled in Romeo's face.

Romeo just looked to the ground.

"You think you're better than me, boy? Do you?"

"No," Romeo said.

"What? I can't hear you? What?" David Kelly said.

"No. I don't," Romeo said, "Just leave me be, please."

That wasn't good enough for the Kelly boy...he laughed and turned and pushed Romeo hard as he could. Romeo hit the ground, his books flying. My group laughed so hard. I said nothing but my mind screamed.

When everybody had their fun and left, I went to Romeo. "Let me help you," I said. I started to pick up his books and papers from the dirt.

"Leave me alone," he said.

"Let me help."

"No, go away." He had anger and hate in his eyes.

I missed the bus to take me home that day. I walked the three miles to my house, thinking and crying. When I got within sight of my house, I saw Granny standing at the end of our drive. She started walking to me.

"Oh gracious! Where have you been?" she asked as she approached me.

"Why didn't you and Papa tell me," I said. "Why?"

"Tell you what, Caroline?"

"Why didn't you tell me that people were so mean. Why?" I held onto Granny and cried some more. "They were picking on Romeo and I didn't help him. I didn't stick up for him."

"People can be mean," she said. "But you don't have to be. You know what's right and what's wrong. You stay true to your heart, no matter what, you hear me? Don't change to please others. The world off this old farm is different, but you don't have to be, ever."

Romeo and Me

10

I decided I didn't need a lot of friends. I didn't mind being picked on by the mean girls... it was better than being one of them. I was happier now. Romeo still ignored me but that was okay. I sometimes would catch sight of his eye and smile at him and think I would see a quick smile back. That's the way it was now. That's the way it had to be.

Papa tapped on my bedroom door.

"You've got company," he said. I jumped up.

"Who?" I walked into our living room and there stood Romeo and his daddy. "Romeo! I said. "Hello!"

"I've come to tell you goodbye, Caroline. Me and Mama are moving up north with Daddy."

"Moving?" It hit me right in my gut. Even though we didn't talk anymore, I still loved the thought of him being just right down the road from me... my best, best friend.

I brought you something. He handed me the picture he had drawn of Queen Amina, on that hot summer day under the shady tree, not that long ago.

"I love this picture. Thank you. I'm going to miss you, Romeo," I said.

"I'm going to miss you, too, Caroline." He walked to me and gave me a tight hug. I hugged him back.

"I love you," I said, and I meant it.

"I love you, too. You're my best friend, Caroline."

Papa and Marcus shook hands, and Marcus promised to send an address so we could stay in touch.

Romeo rubbed his eyes to stop the tears and I let mine flow.

"Wait, I said... I've got something for you, too."

I ran to my room and took the old photograph stuck in the corner of my mirror. It was of two little barn babies hugging and smiling. It was me and Romeo in our own perfect world.

"Keep this to remember me... to remember us," I said.

"I miss those times," he said. "But I won't ever forget them. Thank you."

"Let's go, son," Marcus said. And out the door they went.

Romeo turned and gave me one last smile and wave. It took my breath away, because somehow I knew...

I knew that that would be the last time I ever saw him.

About The Author

Jennie Ford is a mother, writer, potter, and artist. Jennie was raised in Eastern North Carolina, where the rich farming landscapes provide the backdrop to many of her stories.

As a contributor to Storyshares for many years, she will continue to compose short stories for their expanding library. Now residing in Western North Carolina, Jennie is currently writing a novel for young adult readers, which she hopes to publish in the future.

Romeo and Me

About The Publisher

Story Shares is a nonprofit focused on supporting the millions of teens and adults who struggle with reading by creating a new shelf in the library specifically for them. The ever-growing collection features content that is compelling and culturally relevant for teens and adults, yet still readable at a range of lower reading levels.

Story Shares generates content by engaging deeply with writers, bringing together a community to create this new kind of book. With more intriguing and approachable stories to choose from, the teens and adults who have fallen behind are improving their skills and beginning to discover the joy of reading. For more information, visit storyshares.org.

Easy to Read. Hard to Put Down.

Romeo and Me